LEO'S JOURNEY

CERBERUS

GORGON

ATHENS

TEMPLE
OF
POSEIDON

NEMEAN

HARPY

LION

HYDRA

Brownstone's Mythical Collection
A Brief History

For thousands of years, the Brownstone family have tasked themselves with protecting and collecting mythological artefacts and creatures. Now their stories are finally being compiled by me, Professor Brownstone. Contained within these pages, and the books listed below, are my accounts of their great adventures.

Arthur and the Golden Rope
Marcy and the Riddle of the Sphinx
Kai and the Monkey King
Leo and the Gorgon's Curse

This paperback edition published in 2021
First published in 2020 by Flying Eye Books,
an imprint of Nobrow Ltd. 27 Westgate Street, London, E8 3RL.

Text and Illustrations © Joe Todd-Stanton 2020.

Joe Todd-Stanton has asserted his right under the Copyright, Designs, and Patents Act, 1988, to be identified as the Author and Illustrator of this Work.

13 5 7 9 10 8 6 4 2

Published in the US by Nobrow (US) Inc.

Printed in Poland on FSC® certified paper.

MIX
Paper from responsible sources
FSC® C163799
FSC
www.fsc.org

ISBN: 978-1-83874-039-9
www.flyingeyebooks.com

— JOE TODD-STANTON —

BROWNSTONE'S MYTHICAL COLLECTION

LEO and the Gorgon's Curse

FLYING EYE BOOKS
London | Los Angeles

As soon as Leo was old enough to fend for himself, his parents sent him away to study in the great city of Athens. Famous for being the centre of mythological knowledge and learning, they decided it was the perfect place for a young Brownstone.

t one time, the city was under constant threat of destruction
t the hands of countless mythical creatures.

That was until the great goddess of wisdom and war, Athena, became
its protector. She would stop at nothing to keep her Athenians safe.

Athena was proud of the safe city she had created. To ensure it stayed this way, she trained up heroes and sent them on epic quests to protect it.

The Greek heroes were worshipped by the people of Athens for their bravery, strength and skill.

As a student of mythology in Athens, Leo had many classes ...

... but his parents had forbidden him from taking part in the one class he wanted to do more than any other.

All the other students undertook "hero training", so they might become one of Athena's champions themselves one day.

Leo longed to become a her

However, he was always taught that a Brownstone's mission and motto was to "protect mythological creatures", not to fight them.

A fact he was reminded of every day by the pin his parents gave him before he left home.

So Leo kept to his studies ...

... but no matter how hard he tried, he could never forget his dream.

He decided to come up with a plan.

He'd heard Perseus was headed to Athena's temple early the next morning, so before he was called to his first class he sneaked away.

All he wanted was to hear the epic quest that Athena was going to give the great hero.

There have been sightings of Cetus, an enormous, deadly sea serpent, near Poseidon's temple. If you can bring me back a sign that it won't be causing us any more trouble, you will be richly rewarded.

Leo knew he should go back to his room, but his curiosity took hold of him. He wanted to witness a real adventure so much.

The journey to Poseidon's temple was long and treacherous.

And Leo soon started to regret his decisio

hen he tripped.

23

As Leo came to, he saw a huge dark shape in the distance.
It was the dreaded sea serpent that Athena had spoken of!

Leo didn't know what to do. This was a giant, menacing creature who coul
destroy him in a second — but it was also his chance to prove himself.

ustering all of his might and steeling himself for an
pic battle, he ran headlong towards the creature ...

... and then promptly cowered in fear.

All seemed lost until he noticed someone appear behind the monster ...

... and gently remove the arrow from its ta

In an instant, the sea serpent relaxed.

Leo couldn't believe it. The sea serpent had completely transformed.
It didn't look like it would be causing anyone any trouble ever again.

e thanked the girl for saving him and, as a token of his gratitude,
gave her the only valuable thing he had — his pin.

Then, knowing he would have to explain himself
back in Athens, he took the arrow to show Athena.

As soon as he got back, he tried to find Athena to tell her the whole story. However, once the Athenians saw the arrow, they made up their own minds about what had happened.

And suddenly Leo wasn't just Leo anymore. He was...

By the time Athena threw a celebration in his honour, it became
harder and harder for him to ever imagine telling her the truth.

31

From that day on, Leo was no longer just a student of mythology, he was a hero.

eople began to treat him differently and it wasn't long before Athena
alled on him herself, this time to give him a quest of his very own.

The Ceryneian Hind, a gigantic magical deer, has been eating our crops. Make sure this doesn't happen again.

Leo boldly took on the challenge, eager to prove that
he really was the hero Athena believed him to be.

Though try as he might, he could never forget the promise he h[a]
made to his parents. He could never harm a mythical creature.

He had to come up with a more inventive way to complete Athena's challenge.

Athena, impressed by his skills, called on Leo to get rid of more and more mythical creatures. Meaning he had to come up with more and more ingenious ways to get the creatures safely away from Athens.

Leo captivated the Sphinx by making it a toy from his spare quills.

He used tasty treats to lead the Minotaur deep into the dark maze of the wood

He stopped the Cyclops stomping on livestock by fashioning him a special monocle.

He used Pegasus as bait to lure the fearsome Hydra back to the marshes.

He returned Cerberus to the Underworld using nothing more than a giant stick.

He teased the Nemean lion with the impossible-to-unravel Gordian Knot.

And finally, he managed to stop the Harpies from stealing Athens' food supplies by teaching them to fish.

The more monsters he removed from Athens, the bigger his fame grew.

His classmates soon became distrustful. How could Leo be a great hero when he'd never even taken part in one lesson on swordplay or wrestling? Their gossip spread quickly.

nd Athena had some suspicions of her own...

So, she came up with a plan to work out Leo's loyalties once and for all.

The Gorgon is a terrible fiend that can turn any mortal it looks upon to stone. It has found its way to Poseidon's temple and it could attack Athens at any moment. I want you, Leo, to find this monster and bring me back its head. If you do this, you will be the greatest hero Athens has ever known.

Leo left Athens with a heavy heart. His lies had gone too far and now he could see no way out.

He found the path he had taken all that time ago and followed it back to Poseidon's temple.

Readying himself for what was sure to be a dangerous mission, he entered.

To avoid the same fate as previous heroes, Leo used the polished side of his shield to see, then quietly stalked through the darkness.

Until he spotted a shape in the shadows.

The Gorgon was sleeping — this was his chance! It was now or never.

He raised his sword...

But just as he was about to drop it, a glint from the Gorgon's clothing caught his eye. He couldn't believe it – his pin!

Suddenly everything came back to him. How cou[ld] he even dream of harming another creature?

The clatter of his sword hitting the stone floor woke the sleeping Gorgon and, despite how different they'd both become, they recognised each other immediately.

The Gorgon explained to Leo that one day, after meeting him, Athena had caught her helping another mythical creature she had found wounded near Athens.

As a punishment for putting the city in danger, Athena cursed the girl, making her turn any living thing she looked upon to stone.

Now any creature she tried to help, she harmed instead

Ashamed and afraid, she hid herself away in this old temple and tried her best to avoid all living beings.

Leo was in complete shock. Everything he had believed about Athena and her heroes became confused in his mind.

Suddenly a voice boomed through the temple.

Now I see where your true loyalties lie, Leo the so-called "Serpent Slayer". If you won't help me protect my people, then I will have to protect them from you instead!

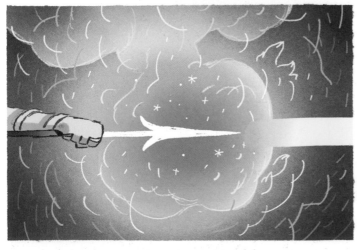

a blind rage, she blasted Leo and the Gorgon far out into the Aegean Sea.

Once again, the mighty Athena was victorious ...

... or so she thought.

A huge dark shape rose up out of the water and loomed over Athena, ready to protect Leo and the Gorgon.

But even with the now fully-grown Cetus on their side, they knew they were no match for such a great and powerful goddess.

Luckily, they weren't alone.

The Gorgon, Leo and the other mythical creatures
decided they would let Athena go on a few conditions...

From that day forward, Athena promised to be more
accepting of the mythical creatures of Greece.

And in turn, they promised never to damage Athens
or harm Athena's beloved people again.

Athena lifted the Gorgon's curse and allowed the girl to use
Poseidon's temple as a place to help wounded monsters.

Leo went back to his lessons and even started teaching some of his own:

How to deal with
mythical creatures
(without harming them)

It proved to be quite popula

And instead of spending his free time idolising heroes,
he decided it was much better spent helping a friend instead.

THE END

ANCIENT GREECE

MINOTAUR

CYCLOPS

MACEDONIA

MOUNT OLYMPUS

TROY

AEGEAN SEA

GREECE

ASIA MINOR

DELPHI

THEBES

CORINTH

ATHENS

SPARTA

SEA OF CRETE

CRETE

CERYNEIAN HIND

CETUS

SPHINX

LEO'S JOURNEY

ERBERUS

GORGON

ATHENS

TEMPLE
OF
POSEIDON

NEMEAN

HARPY

LION

HYDRA